Reflection Dawn

Ed. Iram Fatima 'Ashi'

TANEESHA PUBLISHERS

Title : Reflection Dawn

Editor : Ed. Iram Fatima 'Ashi'

Edition : First (November, 2024)

ISBN : 9789348037770

Published by

TANEESHA PUBLISHERS | *A Venture by -* **PRACHI DIGITAL PUBLICATION**

Regd. Add.: 254, Khuriyakhatta No. 10, Bindukhatta,
Lalkuan, Nainital - 262402, Uttarakhand, India
Website : www.taneeshapublishers.in
E-mail : taneeshapublishers@gmail.com
Phone : +91 845481 2712, +91 976041 7980

Printed by :
Manipal Technologies Limited, Bengaluru - 560001, Karnataka

Reflection

Index

Hope begins in the dark, the stubborn hope that if you just show up and try to do the right thing, the dawn will come. You wait and watch and work: you don't give up.

Anne Lamott

Dear Readers,
Greetings!

Dawn, a whispered promise in the hues of the morning sky, unveils a canvas of hope and renewal with each gentle stroke of sunlight. Where the morning sky whispers promises, our publication unfurls a canvas of hope and renewal with every tender stroke of sunlight. This silent emergence signals the transition from darkness to the golden embrace of a new day.

Witnessing the heartfelt response from our community of poets, authors, and artists is nothing short of overwhelming. It brings me great joy to share the invaluable contributions of these creative minds, including a soul-touching story by Dr. Tarana Yasmin from Patna and Dr. Ratan Bhattacharjee, alongside the poignant verses of Shahid Khan, Muzzammil Shah, Smrutikant Nayak, Gulafshan Salam Khan, Ms. TilKumari Sharma from

Nepal, Ilona Lakatos from Hungary, Binod Dawadi, Aparna Mukherjee and the remarkable artwork of both national and international talents.

Within these pages, readers will be treated to an engaging interview with Elizabeth Esguerra Castillo—an international author, poet, and visual artist. Special gratitude extends to those international poets and artists whose unique contributions have enriched our publication with their exceptional poems and paintings.

Heartfelt thanks are extended to our dedicated editors, associate editors, and artists whose unwavering support has been instrumental. The meticulous layout and vibrant designs, spearheaded by Mr. Vikrant and his team, add a captivating dimension to this issue.

Iram Fatima 'Ashi'
(Editor-in-Chief)
Saudi Arabia (NRI)

Life's Darkness Can Turn Into Light

❖ **Dr. Tarana Yasmin**

Dr Tarana Yasmin from Patna, she is a dentist, writer and director of a school, writing is her passion.

Piyush Chawla, a hero, a warrior and was a man who used to save the life of others. He was a firefighter. Living in a small town of Jammu, he engaged all the time to save the lives of those who used to get stuck in those hilly areas. He had no fear so was he famous for his bravery. Everybody used to respect him in his village. He was 38 years old, married, and was a father of two beautiful daughters. He loved his family very much.

One day as he was about to have lunch, he got a call from one of his friends that there had been a terrorist attack at one of the places near his house. Many people got injured. As he listened this, he left his home hurriedly without informing anyone at home. He didn't inform any one at home but left the house. He reached at of blast spot and saw many people injured and lost their lives. He went to the injured ones and tried to lift them to hospital. He saved the lives of as much many as he could without knowing anyone's identity, any one's name. He wished to see everyone alive. Among them was one of the terrorists Piyush saved him being unaware of his identity. He helped him, saved him and took him to the place the next day wherever he asked him to take. He did everything for the sake of humanity. But that man was a terrorist. He went to the place along with Piyush where he planned the next bomb blast. But without any knowledge, Piyush helped him the way he asked for. Next day, Piyush got the call from his friend that another bomb blast took place at the location where he went yesterday and many people lost their lives. Listening to this, Piyush was shocked.

He went to the place and having seen many dead bodies he felt helpless and guilty as if he had done something wrong. When the Police investigated, they got some clues against Piyush and they arrested him thinking him a terrorist. Piyush was in so much deep shock that he couldn't even open his mouth. Everybody asked him to speak the truth. But he went in deep silence. Everybody started considering him a culprit and started to maintain distance from him. The man who was once a hero for others, who was a life savior once, now became a criminal and terrorist. Everybody started hating him. He went into deep silence. He didn't answer anyone about what had happened that day. As days passed, his life in jail was going on in deep agony.

One day he met the same man in jail whom he saved on blast day. He recognized him but he didn't say anything to him. He felt something fishy might have happened in jail. He heard the man talking to someone about blast in jail. As Piyush heard this, he thought to save the lives of the prisoners and that will help him to prove his innocence. He informed the jailor over there and they arrested the man. Piyush asked him to speak the truth. Piyush knew about his family and so with the help of the police, his family turned up and everybody forced him to tell where the bomb was planted. He was worried about his family so he spoke the truth and the police became successful in diffusing the bomb. He told everything about the one for whom he worked. Piyush asked him to tell the truth about what had happened the day Piyush had been arrested. He told everything how Piyush saved his life and how he trapped Piyush and took him to the place where he already planted the bomb. He asked Piyush for his dress and changed his dress saying his dress is life savior. He wore Piyush's dress and asked him to help in repairing the machine which was not working.

He took Piyush's help and planted the bomb over there. Being unaware, Piyush helped him because his life's motive was to help others and save them. Having listened to all the conversation of the Terrorist they got to know Piiyush was innocent and so they released him from jail with all respect. Everyone thanked him for saving lives of the prisoners and others over there He not only saved the jail but life of everyone there. They gave the bravery award to Piyush and again he got the chance to live his life with full respect and dignity. The Dusk of his life turned into Dawn and he stayed happily and respectably along with his family in his town.

In Dawn's Embrace

❖ **Shahid Khan**

In dawn's embrace, the world takes heed;
Behind dark corners, consciences plead.
Hypocrisy howls with haughty grace;
Voices of the oppressed find no place
And rulers belong to the devilish creed.

With tyranny in vogue, war crimes exceed;
Takers of humanity, an extinct breed.
Hope prevails with a call to prayer at any place
In dawn's embrace.

When media defend their sordid case
Projecting innocents as inhuman race.
Their deceitful words - a venomous seed
To grow forest of falsehoods as decreed.
With a call to prayer evil find no hiding place
In dawn's embrace.

Calendar of Love

❖ **Shahid Khan**

From the dawn of January to the dusk of December,
Let our love blossom like an eternal ember.
In spring's embrace, where blossoms bloom,
Let our hearts entwine, dispelling all gloom.

Your big beautiful eyes like serene moonlight,
Lead me from darkness to realms of delight.
Let's frolic madly like the breeze in the trees,
In the garden of love, let's dance with ease.

Your dimpled smile as fresh as morning air,
A harbinger of hope and death of despair.
Through the heat of summer, let our passion ignite,
Just like a bonfire that burns in sultry midnight.

In autumn, leaves cascade to welcome the rain,
One look at your lively face relieves every pain.
In the cobweb of time, where memories are spun,
Let's weave our love story which can't be undone.

In winter's chill, when we look for warm place,
Let our embrace bring us heavenly solace.
Through metaphorical meadows let's roam,

In the paradise of love, let our souls find home.

In the book of our heart let's write such story,
That transcends from earth to heaven in all its glory.
Let's make journey of our love, a tale to remember,
From the dawn of January to the dusk of December.

A Tale of the Angella Princess

❖ **Dr. Ratan Bhattacharjee**

Dr. Ratan Bhattacharjee is at present Affiliate Faculty English Virginia Commonwealth University Richmond Formerly Associate Professor & Chair Post Graduate Dept of English Dum Dum Motijheel College is at present Founder President of Kolkata Indo-American Society (KIAS) www.kias.org.in. He is a Trilingual Columnist cum Poet. Formerly, he was invited as the International Visiting Professor in Fairleigh Dickinson University USA. Besides, he is the Founder Member in International Advisory Board International Theodore Dreiser Society Philadelphia. Winner of many Educational Excellence Award Dr Bhattacharjee is also Author of many anthologies and senior editor of Reflection W&R Mag.

Angella was sleeping deep. She was dreaming of Elsa party. Dadun will send from India her Elsa dress. She is so happy. This year her birthday will be special. Her all best friends will attend her birthday party. They will also dance with her and she will be the prettiest Elsa Princess that day. But Mr. Aby was calling her. Angella calls her dad Babi. But in affection she sometimes calls him Mr. Aby. Angella was surprised when she opened her eyes. She was not dancing, nor have the friends come to the Elsa Party. She sees that she is on her bed. Her favourite Bunny is near her pillow. In her hands there are still the red gloves. She nowadays wears the gloves herself for avoiding her bad habit of thumb sucking. She wants to be a good baby. Her mama says all good girls never suck their thumb. It is a bad habit as germs can go into the mouth if they suck thumb. Angella thinks a lot on this bad habit. She asks some of her friends if they suck thumb. None of them now sucks thumb Angella asks why they don't suck thumb any more.

"Can you sleep without sucking thumb?" She asked Nai Nai, her best friend in the playschool. Nai Nai is not her real name. Her real name is Nianshuang. Angella gave her a name Nai Nai. And Nianshuang was happy to get the new name. Angella wanted to know why her mom gave her that name. Nianshuang did not know it. She asked her parents and they told her name has a meaning. She is a thoughtful and caring sweet girl. Renee loves Nai Nai for her name. She also wanted to know the meaning of her name.

Her mom said her name is Angella Rudhagni. Angella is the little baby angel and Rudhagni is the Fire of Intellect. Angella did not understand such difficult meaning. She says that she is fire. She is a baby angel She knows magic like Elsa. Nai Nai wanted to know where her mom got her.

Angella asked her mom and dad. She came to know that she came from God. Then she was imagining the rest of the story. One night before sleeping she tells her mom a story. Actually, Angella wants to tell stories to everyone. She tells her little stories to her Dadun (Maternal Grandfather) when he came with

Deemama (Maternal grandmother) from India. Angela told the story of kitty, their neighbor's cat. She felt sleepy. But in her dream she saw where she came from. While in the morning tea table she was taking her milk and strawberry she whispered to her mom's ear that she came to know where she came from. Her mom was curious. Angella smiled and said she dreamt last night and saw she was living with God and later she came to the silly Mr. Aby and Mom.

"Silly?" Her mom asked. Angela laughed in a guffaw. In the playschool she told the story to Nai Nai. They both laughed a lot. Nai Nai said, "Did God throw you down on the carpet or the grass in the lawn?" Angella was not sure where she fell. She still imagined it. She said God threw me down on the carpet. So, I was not hurt." Nai Nai accepted the story. She too does not want God be cruel. She loves God. She tells all to God when she feels sad. One day Nai Nai did not get a rose she wanted to buy from the mall. She told secretly to God about the rose. In the evening her father brought for her a rose. Angella loves drawing heart.

She feels sad, she draws heart and colours it. She keeps it in the letter box at the gate of their house. She sometimes keeps it for Babi when he comes late from his office. She does not want her dad to be late in picking her from the playschool. Her Dad says they work more for earning money for arranging her Birthday party.

Angella said to her dad, you guys why don't you come early to pick me from school? I wait for so long here." But when her dad explains, Angella accepts it. She knows her parents work hard for her birthday party. It will be a dream birthday. Her Elsa Dress came from India. It was fabulous. Super cute dress. She likes the long hair and the magic sword.

"Why do you love Elsa so much?" Her teacher asked. Angella says Elsa is a bold Princess. She heard all these from her mom. Elsa is not a real character. She is imagination. But she is the little character, the Snow Queen.

Her eyes are made of ice, shining and glittering. Elsa knows magic. She can create ice and snow. Anna is her sister. Angella wants to have a sister. But she feels bad if her daddy and mom love that sister more. She wants to be a Princess like Elsa. When Dadun came from India she played a lot of the Elsa game and showed her magic.

Angella's Mom was ready for going to the airport. Angella finally woke up and saw even Dad was wearing his dress for going outside. Today Dadun and Deemama will leave for India. They will go to India and send for her Elsa Dress. So, Renee did not feel sad when they sat in the car.

She sat in between Dadun and Deemama. She asks what else they will send for her on her birthday. She did not want Dadun and Deemama leaving their home. But if they did not go, Elsa dress will not come from India. She won't be able to dance like Elsa. She dreams so many times of Elsa Party in their new home. Angella wants to be the princess. But her mom says that she will be doctor first.

'Shall I be Doctor Princess?" She asked her mom.

Her mom told her, "For us at home you are the Princess, for

all outside you will be a doctor." Angella agrees because she knows Elsa too hides her magic. She will hide her magic wand. She will try to be a doctor. She will study math with her new tutor.

She told dadun, "I have done all my subtraction, all my alphabets and I read five books every day." Angella at the age of four got the certificate of reading one thousand books. Angella told it Nai Nai and Elle. One day Claire called her from New Jersey. She told her about the Elsa Party. She did not tell her the secret story of being Doctor Princess.

She keeps it a secret. She will be doctor for all others and for her family Virginia Princess. She loves New Jersey but as she now lives in Virginia, she wants to be Virginia Princess. Life at Virginia residence is so funny. Angella loves funny people. She never wants any one to be sad.

In the car Angella felt a little sad as they were reaching the Washington Airport. She asked Dadun, "Will you go to India today?" Dadun told how the plane will take high up in the sky. When next day she will wake up, Dadun and Deemama will reach India. Suddenly Angella felt that Dadun and Deemama should not go to India.

Her mom said, "If they don't go how will they send for you the Elsa Dress?" Angella did not reply. Her eyes were full of tears. She said, "I don't want Elsa Dress. I want only Dadun and Deemama. Dadun is so funny. I don't want him to leave me. I want to play with him more and more forever." Dadun gave her a small gift. It was a unicorn. Angella was a little excited to see the glassy eyes of the unicorn. She loves the gift. But still, she cannot accept that Dadun will leave for India. Angella knew if they board the plane, it would take them to India and she would not be able to play the hare and tortoise game anymore. One day she was playing hare and tortoise game. Angella became the hare.

Dadun said," If you become the hare, you will not reach earlier. The tortoise will become first. "Angella smiled. The game started. The hare started running. Dadun was the tortoise. He was going slowly. But as in the story, the hare did not sleep on the road. Dadun said, "You are the hare. You must sleep". Angella said naughtily, "When I am hare, I won't stop." Dadun could not but laugh at Angella's intelligence. This is a new story of Aesop. Here the hare does not stop on the road. These games were very much liked by Angella.

Now Dadun is leaving. Those games she cannot play anymore. She won't be able to do biking every evening. Nor she can go the park now and then. And the running to the hill. Actually, it was an upward road. Angella and Dadun used to climb up the road and run fast. Dadun was a strong old man but dadun cannot still catch her. All these came to her mind. The car sped up and finally reached Washington Airport. Angella became sadder. She could not crack jokes. Nor she laughed when dadun told her jokes.

She is not Elsa. She could not do any magic. She is the real Angella. Real Elsa cannot do any magic to keep her dadun at her home for ever. She said, Dadun please don't leave me. I don't need any Elsa from India. You live here forever." Tears filled her big brown eyes. Angella saw tears in Dadun's eyes too. The security gate comes. Dadun made some video with her but she did not get any fun out of it. She imagines Dadun flying through the blue sky. She will have to go home alone sitting behind on the baby seat. Babi will drive and mom will sit in front. May be mom will come behind to sit with her. At the last moment, Dadun gave her a talking puppy.

She wanted to be happy with that. But Angella could not feel happy with that. She felt like weeping. But dadun told her to be a bold Elsa. Bold Elsa does not weep. Angella is not the Elsa of imagination. Real Elsa might have wept to see her dadun going to India. She wants to be the real Elsa and wanted to weep long. Dadun and deemma gave her warm hugs and kisses. Deemama kissed her belly button. But still tears were coming to her big eyes which cannot fully hold the huge drops.

They trickle down her white cheeks; Dadun and Deemama were waving their palms. But her eyes were wet with tears and her vision became hazy. They came out of the airport and the she sat on the baby seat. She was weeping. Mom gave her chocolates, toys and other gift. The puppy was talking when switched on. But nothing made her sadness lesser. At one time Angella fell asleep weeping.

She was dreaming of Elsa. Dadun sent Elsa from India and her all friends came to her Elsa Party. She was dancing and dancing with the magic wand in her hand, her long hair ponytail swung on the head pulled away from the face, gathered and secured at the back of the head. The car reached their Glen Allen residence when her mom was calling her "Angella, Wake up mama. We are again back to our home".

Interview : Elizabeth Esguerra Castillo

❖ **By Iram Fatima 'Ashi'**

Elizabeth Esguerra Castillo, International Author/Poet/Visual Artist Elizabeth Esguerra Castillo, Professional Feature Writer/Journalist/Blogger and Published International, Author and Poet, Ambassador of Peace and Goodwill to the Philippines for Naciones delas Letras and Semillas Juventud (Argentina), Multi-awarded Published International, Author/Poet/Visual

Artist, Doctor of Literature, Doctor Honoris Causa Recipient, Founder/CEO of Art Heals by Elizabeth Esguerra Castillo, Founder/Owner of Special Quill English, Writing, Editing, and Coaching Services, President CIESART (Camara Internacional de Escritores y Artistas) Philippines Headquarters, Member, Board of Directors of the Illustrious Council of the Presidency of CIESART, President, P.L.O.T.S- Creatives Magazine, USA, Cultural Ambassador to the Philippines for Inner Child Press International, Member, American Authors Association (AAA), Member, PEN International, Member, Asia Pacific Writers and Translators (APWT), Member, World Association of Authors and Researchers (WAOAR), Author, "Seasons of Emotions" (UK), "Inner Reflections of the Muse" (USA).

Can you share with us a bit about your journey as an international author, poet, and visual artist? How did you embark on this creative path?

Writing has always been my first love and I became passionate in writing since my grade school days. I started composing poetry at the age of 10 years old being an introvert. In grade school, I often write love poems and one of my essays in our mother language along with my poem got published when I was 19 years old in a supplementary magazine for high school students "Blue Collar Magazine" of Don Bosco Technical School which circulated nationally.

I believe that because of my quiet temperament, I was able to express myself well in written pieces than in spoken or orally. I had my big break in writing when I became a News Correspondent for a local community newspaper in our city "Antipolo STAR" in 2006 and then I also worked as a Feature Writer for a corporate magazine "Highlights Magazine" for then MMLDC (Meralco Management and Leadership Development Center) before and is now known as First Pacific Leadership Academy.

It was in 2011 that I started getting involved with international anthologies after joining poetry groups on Facebook. The first international anthology which featured my dark poetry that time was based in the United Kingdom. The rest is history since I lost track of the exact number of international anthologies I am in but I do know that it is now more than 200 international anthologies I co-authored.

After winning poetry competition in the UK my prize was a free publication of my poetry book and so in 2013, I published my first book "Seasons of Emotions" published by Destiny to Write Publications, UK. My second book "Inner Reflections of the Muse" was published in 2014 by Inner Child Press International based in the USA again for free because it was a form of compensation for being an Editor and Contributing Writer for their Inner Child Magazine.

Since then, I have been part of a lot of international anthologies and my works were published globally in different literary platforms both online and physical magazines, journals, and newspapers.

Your list of achievements is impressive. What inspired you to pursue a Doctorate in Literature, and how has it influenced your creative work?

I received my Honorary Doctorate (Doctor Honoris Causa) in Literature from the International Literature and Art Academy based in Ukraine. Being chosen to receive this recognition in a vast sea of fellow creatives makes me feel humbled and truly in gratitude and has also ignited more fire in my creativity.

I always tell people around me that I am only in competition with myself and no one else. I just happen to utilize and share the talents and gifts given to me. I believe that they should benefit not just myself but also the whole of humanity.

Being the President of CIESART Philippines Headquarters and a member of the Board of Directors, what initiatives or projects are you currently involved in to promote literature and art in the Philippines?

As the appointed President of CIESART Philippines Headquarters and a member of the Illustrious Presidential Board of Directors, I already started initiatives involving both literature and art. Since last year, I have organized Art Contests and Exhibits for fellow artists and young, aspiring artists. I have collaborated also with different art groups and organizations for upcoming international projects.

We also have been sending open call for submissions to international anthologies not just to members of CIESART but also to other creatives who are willing to join.

My own brand, Art Heals by Elizabeth Esguerra Castillo also gets to mentor and promote young artists not just from the Philippines but from other countries as well. I already have 2 Youth Brand Ambassadors who already participated in international art exhibitions in Turkey and Busan, South Korea. I also collaborate with different art groups for outreach programs.

What inspires your creativity, and can you walk us through your creative process when working on a new piece of writing or art?

I believe that I was born a creative and I also go to harness my writing and art talent through past experiences and observation. I consider myself as an Intuitive Artist. I write about anything when I want to express myself and my views about something, when I want to inspire people through my words.

Are there any upcoming projects or initiatives you are particularly excited about or would like to share with your readers and the literary community?

I am a Participating Artist for upcoming group art exhibitions here in the Philippines and in international exhibitions, both online and offline.

"Verses of Meraki", my poetry collaboration book with Shahid Abbas from Pakistan is also due to be published soon this 2024 in the USA. It is a collection of our poetry duets plus our individual compositions.

I am also working on my third book, "Ver's D Ambedo", a collection of my new compositions which depicts mystical poetry.

Please share your writing experience - the age you started writing and what inspired you to write.

I can say that I already knew what I would become when I grow up even at the tender age of 5 years old. Being an introvert, I would have lots of time to do things all by me and can express myself well in writing than speaking. I have always loved writing ever since I was in grade school. I composed love poetry mostly when I was younger and wrote essays about anything under the sun. Being an observer has taught me many things about the people and my surroundings. With these I can write about anything I am interested in. I am a nature lover and I love looking at the sunset, stars, and moon.

It was after high school that I got to publish my poetry and essay in our mother language in a supplementary magazine for high schools "Blue Collar Magazine" which circulated nationally

Tell us something about your professional life and any other hobby of yours.

Besides being a Professional Writer, I also work as an English Language Instructor for Koreans. I also edit their essays and guide them through their English Writing. I also have my small writing business "Special Quill English, Writing, Editing Coaching Services" and I offer article writing, Press Releases, Artist and Author Interview Services, Book Reviews, Book Promotions, Social Media Management Services, etc. I also write art exhibit titles and art exhibit statements, artist BIO, etc. I cater to both local and international authors and artists, as well as entrepreneurs, life coaches, motivational speakers, among others.

Writing is a medium to express one's inner feelings. Is there any

specific moment or event that made you write?

They say we should not just write when we are inspired. We just write no matter what. What prompts me to write? At certain times when I need to have an outlet to pour out my emotions on paper if I cannot express it verbally. I may write when I am inspired by a song played on the radio, when I see something interesting across the sky like beauteous formation of clouds, a dreamy sunset while walking or when I am out with my friends in some place; when I grieve over something or someone, after watching my favorite movie, etc.

What is your favorite topic to write on? And do you have a specific writing style?

I used to compose mostly love poems, but I believe that my writing evolved through the years. Now, I write about global issues in my own writing style, mystic and metaphysical poetry, current controversial issues, and even protest poetry.
I consider my writing style likened to that of James Joyce' "Stream of Consciousness." My pieces seem to make my readers feel like the character describes them and touches their emotions and core. I can remember two of my constant readers a fellow Filipina and a foreigner who told me that they cried after reading my poems. It kind of "hit" them subconsciously and so they caught themselves shedding tears. Others would send me a message and ask me: "Was your poem written for me?" For

a writer and poet, hearing these words would make us feel fulfilled as we have "moved" our readers in ways we cannot imagine!

Please share who is your favorite writer/poet?

My favorite poets are: Elizabeth Barret Browning, Pablo Neruda, Emily Dickinson, to name a few. For my writing influence, it is Paolo Coelho. All of them have their own writer's voice and style I truly admire. For the metaphysical essays that I write, I am inspired by Coelho's style which is more on the spiritual side of things.

According to you what are the most important elements of good writing?

One's writing should be well-organized, well-researched, grammatically correct, and coherent, should also consider his target audience or readers, and must be written from the "heart."

Please share did you always receive full appreciation and support for your talent in writing in your own family and friends?

Well, at first after telling my parents that I wanted to become a writer and painter that time when I was just in grade six, they were against me taking up Journalism or Fine Arts in college.

Their reason was that there was no money in these careers. I still cannot make them understand that I am not after the money first and foremost but to be able to share my God-given talents to the world. But when I grew up, graduated from college, and started working in corporate jobs, I still felt this emptiness inside me. I decided to pursue what I really love then years after and I felt so complete and fulfilled! I made my loved ones understand and made them proud of my writing and art achievements that I accumulated through the years.

According to you what is the best thing about being an author?

For me, the best thing about being an author is to be able to express yourself in words and share your views about the world with others. Authors can leave a legacy long before they are gone by the pieces or books they have left behind. These never grow old with time.

Since you are a young author and inspiring personality, what advice would you give to emerging authors?

To young and aspiring authors out there, do not stop dreaming. You can fulfill your goals by having a positive mindset. Continue harnessing and improving your writing skills, do not be afraid to try, to get rejected. These are all part of the growth process. My writing journey is not always a bed of roses, either. But the obstacles and hurdles along the way honed me and my potential and brought me to where I am now. Do not get distracted with the "noise", just focus on your goals and believe in yourself.

This time our issue is on 'Dawn', so please share your personal views and sentiments on this topic. Give your opinion on Reflection magazine and would you like to give any advice for improvement?

"Dawn" can depict a diverse range of topics. It can mean waking up to a brand-new day or brand new tomorrow full of hope in the things to come. Seeing the light of day during the early hours of the morning, one feels recharged after having a good night's sleep. Some people are used to waking up very early at dawn to be able to do many things for the day. As the quote goes: "The early bird catches the worm."

"Dawn" may also mean fresh beginnings, fresh talents being discovered, or fresh ideas being brought to the table.

"Reflection Magazine" is already fabulous as it is but new sections involving young and aspiring artists and their interviews would also be wonderful. We can help promote their works and make them know in the international scene.

It is with great joy that I receive your kind words, and I am truly honored to be a source of inspiration for budding artists in the art of writing. May the radiance of your enthusiasm continue to illuminate the creative paths of those who embark on the journey of a[illegible]xpression. Wishing you and all aspiring writers boundless creativity, unwavering perseverance, and the fulfillment of your literary dreams. Profound thanks to you!

Pain Of The Innocents

❖ **Iram Fatima 'Ashi'**
(Saudi Arabia, NRI)

In a world torn by strife and despair,
Where innocent souls cry out in the air,
I close my eyes to the rivers of red,
The dunes of the fallen dead and the tears that are shed.

I wish to shield my ears from the cries,
The bombings, the gunshots, the shattered skies,
But my heart is heavy, my conscience awake,
For the pain of the innocent, I can't forsake.

They label fighters as terrorists, it is not true,
But deep down I know, there's more to their view,
A struggle for justice, for rights and for peace,
In the face of oppression, they strive to release.

I yearn for the comfort of my cozy abode,
To believe in a war, neatly packaged and sold,
But the truth is, it's a conflict untamed and wild,
Where the lives of the innocent are defiled.

I cannot escape the anguish I see,
The widowed, the orphans, the elderly,

Their suffering, their agony, their loss,
It keeps me awake, it's a heavy cross.

I'm bound by the ties of our shared humanity,
To extend my hand, to fight for unity,
For I'm answerable to my Almighty above,
To show compassion, to spread hope and love.

I stand with you, my Ummah, in your darkest hour,
With the strength of your spirit, your resilience, your power,
Free your motherland, I'm standing with, hand in hand,
For a world where peace and justice will forever stand.

The Dawn of Realization

❖ **Aparna Mukherjee**
(Kolkata, India)

Life is full of excitement and rosy moments that what I believed. One day, realization peeks into my heart and everything changes in me. Sun rays of a fresh morning darted in my mind and made me realize where I was wrong. What is the realization? What made me realize?

Hi, I am Sunita who believes in living life to the fullest. I wake up late in the morning. My night starts after 11 pm. I am a college girl who studies in one of the reputed colleges in Mumbai. I am brilliant and I am beautiful which makes me more arrogant. I am quite attractive and all the boys like me. That is what makes me more arrogant. Attitude is my personality. My parents work in the corporate sector. So, I never knew the value of money. Spending money on food parties and on friends is something I love most.

My parents give me huge pocket money every month. If I fall short on money, I ask my dad and he credits to my bank account instantly. Just because I like to spend money on luxurious items or in late-night parties but that does not mean that I am weak in my academics. I notch high grades in semesters which makes my parents and professors feel proud of me. My friends feel equally proud of me.

Life has been a bed of roses for me all this while. I had no idea of responsibility until my dad fell sick. I have been living the life of a queen who has no responsibility and no tension. Whenever I am tense, my dad has always been there beside me who resolves my tensions and worries.

This time, my life has gone for a toss. Everything seems topsy-turvy for me. One fine evening, dad came late in the night because he had an important client meeting along with a presentation. He had dinner late at night. Mom and I had dinner on time around 9 pm. I was waking up late in the night because I had an assignment to submit.

Dad entered the home around 2 am. I saw Dad unlocking the door and somehow, he sat on the couch. I got out of my room and offered Dad a glass of water. He drank half a glass of water and placed the glass on the tablet with tremor hands. I sensed something was wrong. I asked Dad, “Are you OK?” “Yes, beta, I am fine.” Still, my intuition was not agreeing with me.

I sat beside Dad when he was removing his shoes. All of a sudden, he fell off the couch and placed his right hand on the left side of his chest. He was sweating profusely. I started getting jitters. Dad was breathing fast and he experienced severe pain in the chest. I could not understand what to do. I wanted to wake my mom. But, I did not because she has a high blood pressure.

I called up our family physician and told him about Dad’s condition. Doctor uncle said that he was sending an ambulance. By that time, I went to my neighbor’s home and told them about my dad’s critical condition. They came to my house to see Dad. The ambulance arrived in the meantime. My neighbour and the staff members of the hospital took my dad to the ambulance.

My mom got up all of a sudden and started panicking. I tried to calm down my mom and made her believe that Dad will be well. My neighbor, mom, and I reached a multispecialty hospital. Dad was taken in the ICU. We sat outside in the corridor. The cardiologist was assessing my dad's health. Several medical exams had been done. After a while, doctors confirmed that my dad had a mild cardiac arrest.

The timely action taken by me had saved my dad's life. He was in the hospital for three days. Mom was crying on end. It was getting tough to calm down my mom. I was with Mom and made her believe that dad is fine. She was getting more restless. Doctor came outside the ICU and informed us that dad will be under observation the whole night.

Mom and I did not sleep the whole night. Somehow, I made my mom sleep on the chair. I was pacing up and down the whole night. Some good memories shared with my dad were flashing in front of my eyes. That night in the hospital, I rushed to the doctor's cabin thrice to know about the condition of my dad. He made me believe that he is expecting his patient to be fine tomorrow morning. I saw dad with an oxygen mask which I have never seen him in this condition. I held my dad's hand lightly and a drop of my tear fell on his hand. I wiped it slowly so that he did not get disturbed. I walked out of the ICU room slowly, turning back again and again.

Next morning around 5:15 am, a sister who was in the ICU room called the doctor with a loud voice. Mom and I got scared and we rushed into the room. Dad was in a static condition and was breathing slowly. Doctor assessed my dad again and informed us that he was out of danger. He approached me and patted my back and said, "Every girl should be brave and dutiful like you. God bless you."

Mom and I were relieved by his words. In the afternoon, Dad opened his eyes and held my hands tightly. I told Dad not to talk. We are always here with him. He smiled and slept again, as if he was on tranquillizer.

That night made me realize the importance of being responsible. In just one night, life made me realize what responsibility is. The dawn of being a responsible daughter was no less than dawn for me. I am no longer the carefree girl anymore. I understand that I have some responsibilities toward my parents. Life is not a bed of roses. Sometimes, we have to walk on the thorns to come out strong in life.

Dawn

❖ **Dr. Tarana Yasmeen**

When the silence, in the dark
Fades its darkness and spread the light
Birds start chirping
And creates the music
Feel the rhythm
Feel the sound
Turn the darkness

Into the dawn
Starts your day with new hope and ray
Be your fighter
Be your lighter
Burn the Demon
And become the Ram
Be your Lord
Be your Master
Be the guidance
Be the path
Touch the success
And embrace the mark
Be the power
Be the inspiration
Make others feel your worth
Be your hero
Feel the enlightenment
And shine in the light!!

Dawn of Hope

❖ **Muzzammil Shah**

(Muzzammil Shah, he is an English lecturer who hails from Bahraich. He composes poems both in English and Urdu. Presently he enjoys teaching in Buddha Public School Bahraich)

Have still hope to live,
Life doesn't end with an accident,
yet it gives a boost new,
On the way of success, be confident,
Life is colourful, each has its own charm,
some benefit us, but others harm.
A street is not a world in all,

Each road ends at a crossing,
All directions thee humbly call,
Now you to choose one for passing,
The world always witnesses success and failure,
Both are essential for making a skillful life-sailor.

Spoil not yourself for your beloved one,
Even she wants you smile forever,
Many stars are there to be inspired by the sun,
Deprive them of thy light never,
New hope and life say, 'The world is vast,
Come out into the light, leaving your gloomy past.'

"Written In the Stars" (Inspired by the movie "Winter's Tale") They say for each person There is a certain Miracle from within And you are meant to be just for one person As time draws to a close to meeting the One, The Universe and your Spirit Guides are on your side To help you fulf

Innocent Blood

❖ **Elizabeth Esguerra Castillo**
(Philippines)

I can hear the cries of innocent children,
Screaming for justice, for survival
In a cruel world they were born in but never chose.

With eyes longing for a chance to exist
And wake up to a beautiful morning one day
When all these terror around them cease.

Spare the innocence of these young angels
Created out of love, now suffering

From the hands of evil they know nothing of.

Spare the children of Palestine
Almighty God, spare them from this fury
Open the gates of heaven to those who perished
And sacrificed their lives for their faith all for your glory.

Racing Time

❖ **Elizabeth Esguerra Castillo**
(Philippines)

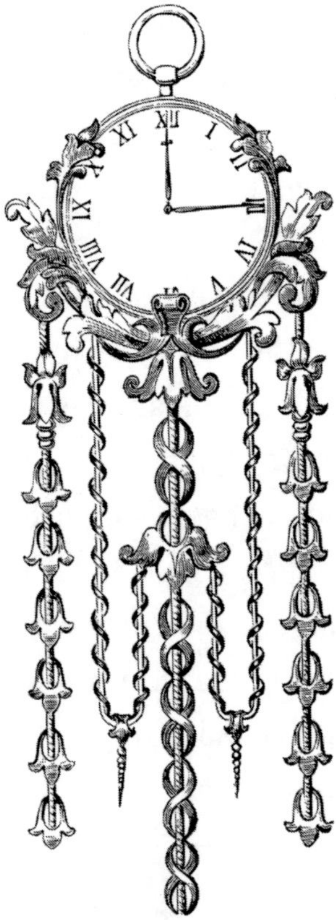

Look at their faces-
Bewilderment written in every crease
Anxiety cracking each vein-
Dark circles around each eyes
Worry engulfing each waking day.
They are racing time-

In a moment that seems frozen
The pandemic gets into their system
Humanity being erased by a single virus.
Racing time, fearing droplets in the air,
Suffocated, panic becoming a hobby
Life pathetically wrapped in worry
Racing time, how can we be fools of our own doing?
Don't you realize evil is tempting our faith?
When fear takes the lead in every move we make?
When the Uninvited Guest- death
Makes us forget the purpose of our life's journey.
Racing time, humanity in a frenzy
Have we abandoned all hope
That instead of living in fear each passing day,
We should spread love and compassion?
We don't have to race with time
And bring everything to a halt,
The Universe is challenging us in a hard way
Not anyone of us knows why.

Rays Of Resilience

❖ **Smrutikant Nayak**

Dawn
A new day
A new hope
A new light
About to be bright...
A new page to the diary of our life.

A reason
To thank the almighty
To smile and forgive
To breathe and forget
To hold it tight
And brace, it's gonna be alright!

A challenge you love
A blessing you seek
A prayer to offer
A poem to share
Something that's new
A lotus with a drop of dew

Dawn brings a new you...

The Dawn

❖ **Gulafshan Salam Khan**

(Gulafshan Salam Khan is an explorer and curious person at heart. Her love for the English language sparked her interest in reading, writing, and art. Currently, she is a PhD candidate in education at RUDN University in Moscow, Russia)

The night came, and knocked at the door
Many hopes were shattered
It was hard to see; the agony marched
Pushed us into a deep well of hopelessness.

In the chaos and silence of life
A little angel stepped at our door
Planted a kiss on our cheek
It made us feel that there is light in the darkness.

It dawned upon us the secret of life
No matter what, dark or light
It is the positive spirit that makes us fly
It is how we live our lives by being grateful.

Appreciate little things in life
The blazing sky or sparkling stars
The running water or chirping bird
The dawn brings hope and erases our fear.

The Morning Dream

❖ **Ms. TilKumari Sharma**

Ms. TilKumari Sharma (Nepal) a Multi Award Winner in writing from the International sector is from Bhorle- Hile, Paiyun 7, Parbat, and West Nepal. She has published many thousands of poems, some essays, stories and other literary writings in International Magazines, groups and anthologies from (amazon.com) Russia, America, England, Hong Kong, Greece, Philippines, Hungary, Brazil, Chile, Scotland, Indonesia, Bangladesh, South Africa, Kenya, Nigeria, North Africa, Trinidad and Tobago, Spain, India, Nepal and many other countries. She is a featured -poet and best-selling co-author too. She is a world-renowned poet now. She has received gold, silver and excellent award from different International groups of poetry. She is a moderator in the Global Poetry Forum. She is the poet of the Guinness World Record Book named Hyper Poem.

Sunshine in dream
Fresh and healthy
The life changes in the worth.
The light of mind
Fresh journey to dream
The life of eternity
The sunshine of morning sleeping
The worth of life going

Smiling and eternality
The life of light and eternal entity
The morning bighting of humanity
Planting kindness in earth
The earth is melting.
The life is in hard struggle.
Dreams awakes me up.
The light of higher life
The dignity in it.
The fine art and artistic creativity
The worth of human life is humanity.

At Dawn

❖ **Ilona Lakatos**

IlonaLakatos (Hungary), she is Marketing and advertising manager. She is engaged in writing and painting. It plans and implements international virtual exhibitions. "Creating People's Side Virtual International Exhibition" (CPS). Founder and manager of a gallery of international artists, International PR Consultant {P.L.O.T.S.} ~Creatives Magazine (USA)
She has published 13 books. Volumes of poetry, e-books made of interviews and film reviews, story books and the novel Lusion. Her writings were also published in anthologies and magazines: Hungary, Slovakia, Italy, Mexico, United States, Trinidad, Bangladesh, India). She won first place in several competitions and received awards. (Beijing Mindfulness Literature Museum 2023 "ZhengNian Cup" Literary Award - Short Story Award).

The birds sing merrily
This is how they welcome the new day.
My tired body also comes to life,
What does the new day promise?

The buses are also ready to go,
people go to work.
They are still a little sleepy,

but they are already looking forward to a new day.
The street is slowly filling up,
everyone goes somewhere.
The children go to school
Some people are in a hurry to go shopping.

The first ray of sunshine
is already stretching its petals.
I feel its warmth on my face
I'm leaving too, it's a nice day.

Dawn

❖ **Mrs. Praveen Gola**

Mrs. Praveen Gola is an online freelance writer and journalist. She is a writer of romance. As writing is her passion, she loves to write Shayari. Some of her poems have been read at the international level. Her poem "MeriPehchaan" was chosen for a film by Yes Foundation India. One of her stories titled "AdhooriAurat" was dramatized by AakhaayanNatshaala in Indore. Another article was published in an Urdu newspaper, "Daily Siyaq," in Pakistan. She worked as a "Delhi representative" with AbhinavBalmann magazine for two years. Many of her poems have been published in Reflection W&R magazine, and she has also been working as an associate editor with this magazine.

In the hush before the sun's first ray,
Dawn breaks the grip of night's cold sway,
A promise whispered in the morning's hush,
Of hope and dreams in a tranquil rush.

The sky, a canvas, painted in pastel hues,
As darkness scatters, morning's light renews,
A world awakens from its slumber deep,
In dawn's tender embrace, secrets we keep.

With each delicate breath, a new beginning's call,
The world unfolds, a tapestry for all,
A symphony of colors, a soft, gentle birth,
Dawn's sweet caress, the most precious of earth.

It cradles the day in its golden hands,
As hope emerges from night's shifting sands,
A fresh canvas painted with dreams anew,
Dawn, the artist, painting skies so blue.

In this quiet moment, a gift we find,
A tranquil refuge for the heart and mind,
Dawn, the harbinger of life's grand design,
A chance to start again, in its embrace, we shine.

Dawn

❖ **Binod Dawadi**

Binod Dawadi, the author of The Power of Words, is a master's degree holder in Major English. He has worked on more than 1000 anthologies published in various renowned magazines. His vision is to change society through knowledge, so he wants to provide enlightenment to people through his writing skills.

You give a new hope for a life,
You make us happier,
When we see you in the sky,
Sun! You are always working all day,

and night like that we should also,
Work hard no matter how many obstacles come,
in the life but we should be stable,
As well as strong,
as a sun,
Sun you are the eye of a God,
Who is truth and who has beauty,
So we should learn many things,
From the sun,
Dawn you call me and,
Tell me that I have a life,
As well as always makes me realize that I am living.

Twittering Dawn

❖ **Promila Bhardawaj**

Promila Bhardawaj, Retired General Manager from the Industries Department of Himachal Pradesh Government, India, is a bi-lingual Poetess whose six Anthologies of Hindi and English poetry have been published while her poems, articles and short stories have been published in National newspapers, national and international literary magazines and many Poetic Anthologies. Besides participating in Literary & Cultural Programs and T.V. Programmes, many citations, awards and appreciation certificates have been rendered to her from esteemed literary institutions and literary- cultural groups.

Twittering of birds, sitting on mango tree
Sing so many sweet songs to wake me,
Cool breezes holding my hand
Compel me to get up from bed,
Patting my cheeks so gently
Caressing my head so softly,
As my mother did affectionately,
Hug me and then take me outside,
Where branches of trees so amusingly nod
That I have to automatically respond,
Laughing flowers cheer me up lovingly
Bringing smiles on my face cleverly,

Inviting me eagerly to come near
As if asking me to adore and admire
Their beauty and colourful dresses,
Attracted by whom soon butterfly comes
To fill fresh enthusiasm in my body
Inspiring me to get ready to fly,
Shunning my lethargy and laziness,
In the vast sky's realm of happiness.
Waiting for me and all to reach there
By working diligently with full fervor.

Mysterious Edward Asylum

❖ **Arohi & Athrav**

There was an asylum outside the city Rajnagar, the asylum was made during the English era and was named after well known psychiatrist Dr Edward. Due to desertion the asylum building was in very bad shape, it was turning into ruins every passing day. The asylum was deserted long ago as there were rumors that the asylum was hounted. People used to say that there were so many powerful and weak spirits in the ruins of the asylum.

People had little Information about this hounted place but there were several stories which explain how this place became hounted. One of the popular stories was that during the late 70s a truck driver Jorawar met a severe road accident; he lost three of his friends who burned alive in the accident. After this accident he became violent and insane. He was lately admitted Eduard Asylum. It is said that one day he became very violent and killed several doctors and patients. During this violence he lost controll and fall from the third floor of the asylum and died. After that day he was often found wandring in the premises of the asylum and people started dying mysteriously.

After observing several mysterious deaths in the asylum goverment officials started investigating into this matter but found nothing. They could not do anything and people went on dying mysteriously. At the beginnig of 1980 the death toll was 150, several doctors and patients had died mysteriously; that was the time when goverment decided to shut this asylum.

The asylum building was evacuated and it was locked forever. Soon some thieves broke into the asylum to steal the equipments of the asylum but they were found dead next day. It was the time when the asylum was declared hounted and people were warned to go near the asylum building. Soon people started hearing screams coming out from the asylum building at night, afraid people started telling bad things about the asylum and people decided to abandon the asylum building.

Trapped In Nowhere

British youtuber Robert Winters decided to celebrate his 17th birthday in India. He along with his friends Jack, Lasso and Ronald planned a car trip in the northeren region of India. His birthday was on 15th October and they arrived in India in the last week of September. Their tour operator provided them a big and comfertable car with a good driver.

They travelled all the big cities of northeren India during the first week of October doing youtubing and enjoying their trip. There destination city for Robert's birthday was Jaigarh. To reach Jaigarh they had to pass through Rajnagar. On 14th October they reaced Rajnagar and Jaigarh was still 350 kilometers away so they decided to travel all through the night. They took their dinner in Rajnagar and left the town at 9o'clock in the evening.

At the outskirt of Rajnagar their car stopped. Their car driver did his best to start the car but the car did not start. The car engin was stalled and there was no signels in their mobiles. There was no way but to go back to the city and find a car mechanic. Their driver Dilawar shrugged and said, "There is no way but to find a car mechanic, I'm going back to the city, you guys better stay near the car, I'll come back as soon as I find a car mechanic."

"Go ahead buddy." said Lasso, "We are fine, we'll camp here untill you came back."

They were stranded and there was a big dark building on the other side of the road.

"Hey guys, look at that building...." said Ronald, "Why should we camp here, we can stay in that building untill the driver come back."

"What the hell are you talking about?" said Robert, "That

building is wrapped in dark, there may be raptiles inside the building, we should camp near this car."

"You are talking like a coward......" laughed Lasso and said, "Birthday boy, this is something new to do on your birthday eve, don't act like a chicken, let's go near that building. We'll just see the building from outside and come back."

Lasso ran towards the dark building and Jack, Ronald and Robert followed him.

Soon they reached the main gate of the building. There was a heavy lock on the iron gate.

"Look guys at the name of the building." said Jack, "Throwing his mobile's torch light on the name of the building written on the top of the gate."

The name was 'Edward Asylum.'

Whispers From The Past

Lasso peeped through the gate and saw there was a veranda behind the main door of the building.

"Guys........it's cold outside....." said Lasso looking at the veranda, "We don't need to go deep inside the building but we can stay in that veranda untill Jorawar brings a car mechanic."

"No......not a good idea; the floor of that veranda should be full of dust and dirt....." said Robert, "I'm not going inside this eerie building, let's go back."

"He is a coward; let's get into the building through that fallen wall." said Jack throwing his mobile torch's light on the fallen boundry wall of the building.

"Yes.....we are going inside....." said Ronald, "Robert will follow us."

Soon they all jumped over the fallen wall and entered the building. That very moment someone screamed inside the building.

"Did you hear that scream?" asked Robert.

"No, we didn't......" said Lasso laughing, "Your ears are playig tricks with you."

After a few moments they entered the main door of the building and stepped into the veranda.

The veranda was full of dust and broken glass, it seemed that no human entered this building for years. To their surprise the atmosphare of that building was very cold.

"Guys, I don't have good feelings about this place." said Robert, "Let's get out of this spooky place."

"Spooky place my foot." said Ronald, "Lets find a room, the room inside the building may be rather hot."

"I'm not going inside the building." said Robert, "I feel there is some unknown entity inside this building which might harm us, please leave this place and sit inside our car."

"Look guys, don't argue....I need to pee right." said Jack, "I'm going inside the building to find a proper pace to pee. I'm just coming back, please wait for me."

"You guys are impossible......" said Robert, "Please don't get lost Jack."

As soon as Jack went inside, they all heard some strange

whisper. All of them peeped through the dark but they couldn't understand what was going on.

How To Survive

Jack went inside the building but he didn't find any proper place to pee. Soon he saw there was a bluish light in a far corner of the corridor. Jack went towards that light and to his surprice there was a teen girl in rags and was eating a rat, her mouth was full of blood. The girls looked at Jack with her firecy eyes.

Jack trembled with fear and ran back towards the veranda, the girl jumped like a cat and ran behind him.

Jack was running like a mad man, he could run no longer, he stumbled and fell on the dirty floor of the corridor. A flying brick fell on his head which crushed his head. He screamed violently and died.

Ronald, Robert and Lasso heard several screams, they were terrified but as Jack was inside the building they could not go out of the building.

"Guys, Jack is in trouble." said Ronald, "I'm going to find him."

Robert and Lasso could say nothing. Ronald left them and entered the corridor. The corridor was dark.

Ronald moved ahead and saw there was big staircase and human figur standing upstair. Maybe he was Jack, Ronald went upstair but there was none.

He looked back, someone was walking slowly in the corridor. Ronald tried to look through the dark and that very moment a heavy object hit his head and he fell dead in the corridor.

Escape

It had almost been half an hour since Jack and Ronald went inside the building. Robert and Lasso were concerned about their safety.

"It has been very long time." said Robert, "Let's go inside and our friends."

"Aren't you afraid of going inside?" asked Lasso, "There might be trouble inside, let's get out of this hell."

"There might be trouble...." said Robert, "But we need to find our friends, we cannot left them here."

Lasso said nothing and he started following Robert who was entering the corridor.

The corridor was dark, there was no light inside, their mobile torches were not working properly but there was some starange light through which they could see things around them.

As they moved ahead they saw the dead bodies of Jack and Ronald and saw an entity which was eating them.

Lasso wanted to scream but Robert cupped his mouth with his hand and whispered to keep quiet.

Robert motioned Lasso to retreat. They ran back and that very moment that entity ran behind them, it was flying in the air instead of walking on the floor. Things like bricks were flying all over them and hitting their bodies.

Soon they were in the veranda and saw the glass door of the main door was shut.

Lasso and Robert were terrified but Robert took a big brick from the floor and hit the glass door with it. The glass of the door broke with a loud sound.

Robert and Lasso ran outside of the building through the broken glass door. They ran towards the fallen wall but there was no falled wall. They saw a hole in the wall on the other end of the building, but they didn't try to go near the hole, it might be a trap. They struggled to climb the six feet wall. They helped each other and jumped over the wall and ran towards the road.

They didn't look back untill they reached the road.

They looked back, the entity inside the building was faded away but the screams inside the building were deafning their ears.

They saw their car driver had come back with a tow away vehicle and was tying the car with it.

"Where are the other boys sir." asked the car driver.

"Died inside the building......" said Lasso with his terrified voice.

The driver looked at them and motioned them to enter their car.

Their car was going back to city and Robert and Lasso were sad about the violent death of their friends. They were thinking about themselves if they were really saved or it was just a bad dream came to en end.

Let me be

❖ **Dr. Ruchida Barman**
(Jaipur, India)

She wanted to scream
But was forbidden
She was fuming with rage
But-Good girls are not supposed to express anger
She was dying to cry out in pain
Pain of hurt, pain of betrayal, pain of loneliness when surrounded by people
But - Good girls have to learn to be quiet
How can they be hurt, they are not supposed to be
She was traumatized by family, friends and at work place
But - Good girls are supposed to be quiet, not tell anyone
So, I am not a Good girl, I don't want to be one
Let me be Bad, but let me Scream, let me express my Pain, let me talk of my trauma
Let me be ME

Man Eaters Of Kali Valley

❖ Kumar Vikrant

Last Hunter

Kunwar Vishal Rana, the seasoned hunter; was a bit frustrated today. Rani the tigress and her fully grown cubs had been playing hide and seek with him for three days. During the last three days, he had a strange feeling that the big cats were around but were not ready to take the bait which he set for them.

He was from the royal family of Devdurg and as his ancestors; he was also a very good hunter. Hunting animals has been forbidden in India long ago, so there were not many chances when he could enjoy hunting. Whenever a lion or tiger becomes man-eater the state governments give him killing assignments, which he takes gleefully, after all, he loves killing those beasts.

Rani and her cubs have escaped from Jill Wilson National Park, situated 500 km east of Kali Valley. Since, the one month of their escape, they have killed so many human beings including renowned Will City industrialist Jag Jindal and his son Viki Jindal, who somehow crossed their path in the wilderness of Kali Valley. Their car driver told to police that while coming back from Devdurg central jail, they felt the urge of urinating and that very moment the three beasts emerged from nowhere and killed his masters.

Powerful Jindal family took the matter to the home minister of India and the three big cats were declared man-eaters. State government invited amateur and professional hunters to kill the big cats after the cats killed the two forest officers who were trying to kill them. Three hunters from Rajasthan royal families took the task of killing the big cats in their hands but all the three hunters were found missing just after three days of their hunt.

After they went missing, there was a price of rupees one crore on the heads of the big cats, but no one dared to go after them.

Finally, the descendant of the former royal family of Devdurg, Kunwar Vishal Rana took the impossible task in his hands, not for money but for an act of valour.

His team with satellite locators was constantly updating him about the whereabouts of the tigers and he was ready with his bait, powerful rifles and 12-gauge slug to meet the beasts. But they were not taking the bait, either they were not hungry or they have sensed the risk.

These dumb cats know nothing but killing and live on their kill, was Vishal's firm belief but these three beasts are acting strangely. Man-eaters don't dwell at the same place for a long time, they are normally on run all the time, but these big cats' satellite images were indicating that they are around since the hunt began. Vishal was constantly in contact with his team, who has camped outside the valley with his satellite phone.

Tracking beasts with satellite is easy but killing them was becoming tougher with every passing day. He was a bit frustrated; he wasn't habitual of living in dusty ravines of this blasted valley. He hasn't taken bath for two days and his body was stinking.

"Update, Moksha," he spoke in Bluetooth speaker connected to his satellite phone.

"They are in the two km circle of your loft and resting." Moksha his wife replied from the camp.

"Damn cats, it's getting darker and your damn satellite monitor doesn't work in the dark. Bait is the only way to lure them; these new technologies are useless in the darkness of night."

"Vishal, why are you so obsessed to kill those beasts; I don't like it all. I advise you to give up and come out of this blasted valley."

"I'm a Rajput, I don't give up so easily; you are from traders family you'll not understand it all."

"I'm also a Rajput, if my family is running so many industries don't make us traders; don't you understand that the professional and government hunters couldn't kill those beasts; what is so special in you?"

"They were not Rajput; that is the difference; these beasts are destined to get killed by me."

"Don't brag, those beasts don't differentiate amongst the clans of humans they recognize them as their prey and kill them."

"Don't teach me about these cats now let me concentrate on the hunt."

"Vishal; please give up, come out, I have had some bad feeling all day today."

"I don't like these feminine willies, please go to the camp and try to catch some sleep, we might have a long night today," said Vishal and disconnected.

Unwanted Hero

"Total six hunters have been killed hunting the runaway tigress Rani and her cubs. The latest killing recorded was hunter Kunwar Vishal Rana, he was killed by the beast trio yesterday night, and his half-eaten body was found in the ravines of Kali Valley." announced the beautiful newswoman with a sinister smile.

In the background, there were blurry images of hunter's remains and his weeping wife's gloomy face.

Jack changed the news channel to get more updates on this latest killing. He was totally confused and surprised to notice this strange behaviour of the man-eater tiger clan. Kali Valley was a playground of bandits and outlaws but now this fugitive tiger clan was surpassing them, their main targets were the men who were trying to kill them. They have crossed hundreds of kilometers of the vast infertile valley but whenever the hunters were around, they'd stay and won't leave the place until they hunt their hunters.

Intelligent cats? No this is not an idiotic Bollywood flick, this is reality, and people are being killed. Thought Jack forgetting his own hatred for the people who kill wild animals just for the fun sake and the killed hunters were not better than them.

Today he had to go to Will City to get grub for the dwellers of his farmhouse. Amelia, his Goddaughter has also come back from her school to pay him a visit and she was desperate to do some shopping in the newly opened mall.

"Hurry Amelia, we got to go now, I have some unfinished business out there, which I have to do at any rate today." Hollered Jack.

"Coming Dad..." a sweet voice came from the farmhouse building.

Next very moment two girls of same age came out of their room to join Jack who was waiting for them in his Ford Classic Jeep. They jumped into the jeep and occupied rear seats.

"Dad we need a car with roof and walls, this open jeep is no better than a roller coaster," said Amelia winking at her friend.

"Top your school, I'll get a sedan for you."

"You are asking for too much dad."

"Then enjoy this roller coaster."

"You are impossible, dad," said Amelia hopelessly.

Jack overheard her and went on driving.

After 30 minutes he stopped the car before the Will City mall and handed Amelia his credit card.

"Enjoy kids; I'll come back in three hours."

"Okay dad......" said Amelia and the girls ran towards the entrance of the mall.

Jack's next destination was Police Headquarter where he went to meet the Deputy Inspector General Rahul Dev, who wasn't happy to see him at all.

"Why Jai, what brought you here?" asked the DIG gruffly calling Jack by his real name.

"I just came to know, what is going on in the valley?"

"What a joke, the keeper of the valley came here to know about the well being of his own playground."

"I'm serious DIG, people are getting killed, and this is not good."

"So the old Jack has become a saint and is worried about the bloodshed. The man, who has filled the valley with dead bodies, is worried about people getting killed."

"DIG sir, I came here to inquire about the hunters who were killed........"

"News people are telling more than we know, go open the TV, you'll know all."

"Who permitted the hunters to kill those tigers, knowing the fact that the tigers shall kill them?"

"I permitted them, you are a good shooter yourself; go kill them and earn the reward of rupees one crore."

"Rubbish, I don't need your advice and money."

"Then why did you come here? Just to check my patience that how long can I bear a prime minister Bravery award holder, the protector of Will City, false God of Kali Valley."

"No, just to advise you to not to send more hunters after the beasts."

"So, now you'll tell me how to handle my duties."

"No, to save some hunters from those tigers. Now I'll go after them."

"That is really good news, go, Jack, get killed and free this city from a false hero. You need some hunting gear? Go contact my orderly, he'll give you everything."

"I don't need anything from you......."

"I know you have all the modern warfare; just let me have a glimpse of that, you'll rot in the jail for the rest of your life."

"Give a try DIG; I'm eager to see that day."

"Now get out, I need to do some work to earn my living; I'm not a millionaire like you."

Jack left the police headquarter.

As soon as Jack left the DIG office, the DIG dialed a number and said to someone, "Beware, now the fool is rushing in and he is a damn good killer. A friendly advice; maintain distance from him otherwise consider yourself dead."

Unwanted Visitors

Jack was surprised to see Central America's drug mafia's killers in the Will City mall. Their names were Carlos Luis, Jose Alejandro and Jorge Eduardo, all three of them were ruthless killers. Their presence in Will City was not just a coincidence, they were after someone. Someone was about to die.

Jack called up his farm manager Raut, who himself was a former contract killer but now living in peace looking after the horses of Jack's stead farm. He was around, Jack gave him instruction to have an eye on them and be in low profile.

Another Hunter

Rajah Manjit Singh, a big burly Sikh was enjoying the horse ride around his big agriculture farm in the outskirt of Patiala, Punjab. It was a sunny day which was almost impossible in late December in Northern India.

Suddenly his horse got restless, he patted him to calm down but the horse whimpered and got more restless. Manjit tightened the rein otherwise the horse would have run in the opposite direction.

Out of nowhere, a wild boar came running from the bushes, the boar was furious and eager to hit the horse. Manjit's hand acted rapidly and he took out a colt magnum revolver from his belt and shot the boar. The boar took the big bullet easily and ran more furiously towards the already jumping horse.

Manjit fired thrice rapidly and that was enough for the boar. It dropped dead just a few feet from the horse.

Manjit called up his farm servants to collect the lunch meat which he killed for them recently.

After thirty minutes he was in his big farmhouse taking bath. On the morning shot of scotch, he went through the newspaper which had a full story on the killer tigers of Kali Valley.

"Interesting..." he murmured; it was a hunting call for him. He just came back from Africa after hunting some illegal big games.

He called his servant and told him to take out his hunting gear; he was going to Will City to have this hunting fun. It was really a long time ago when he killed a tiger for fun sake but now, he'll collect these trophies legally.

"Kali Valley, I'm coming," he said with a smile and called up his traveling agent to make arrangements for his flights and stay in the Will City and Kali Valley.

Game Begins

"Kids; I have some important work tonight. Take your dinner and have rest."

"Dad, please don't go, I don't like you to go after those mad cats," said Amelia with a lot of concern in her voice.

"Amelia another hunter has entered the valley this evening and his life is in danger. I need to save him if possible."

Amelia knew how he fought with police goons to save her; no one can stop him if he has decided to do something.

"Dad will you come back," said Amelia with her moist eyes because she knew if he doesn't return she'll be an orphan again.

"Don't worry kid, I always come back. Now enjoy your stay here, we'll watch your favorite movie tomorrow in your favorite cinema.

"I'll wait dad."

"I'll come back kid."

Rounding Up The Beasts

Manjit knew something fishy was going on in the valley so he had a helicopter survey of the possible whereabouts of the man-eaters. He didn't have a glimpse of them but he knew they were around.

For his loft he selected a steep dune which could give him the clear view of the area around him. No bushes were around, he hates surprises. He had all the big range guns with him including a tranquilizing gun, which was of least use but he did not want any chance with those beasts.

DIG Rahul Dev provided him a team of experts who'll keep him updating about the beasts. Manjit didn't like it at all. He hated people telling him what to do.

Idiots! this is jungle no rules work here only one rule works here which is the survival of the fittest.

He dumps the satellite phone provided by the DIG people, deep in his hunting gear for he wanted no distraction.

There was a bulletproof vest under his long Chester. He saw

the sun setting in the West and the freezing cold took the entire valley in its grip.

The laborer who made twenty feet wide and twenty feet deep ditch around his loft have gone long leaving him and his baits alone in the dreaded valley. The baits were three goats which were bleating nonstop attracting the big cats and other night beasts of the valley.

Lost Kid

Jack took his favourite tranquilizing rifles and their darts. His colt revolvers and cartridge were well kept. He patted his stead Duke and rode on it. He was so confused about the killer trio, Carlos Luis, Jose Alejandro and Jorge Eduardo; who were doing sightseeing and behaving like rich tourists. They were careless, which was strange for the people of their caliber.

"This is the riddle which will solve itself soon." said Jack to himself and entered the dreaded Kali Valley.

His people have told him about the whereabouts of the new hunter and he wanted to be close to him all the night tonight. It was not sure that the cats shall take his bait tonight it might take several nights. Those beasts might turn up in a few moments or might take several weeks. But he had strange feeling that it is going to be a long night for him tonight. He loosened the rein of Duke and next very moment he was running like a whirlwind.

He was in the middle of his journey when he saw a woman sitting in the middle of the road, it was almost impossible to go ahead without hurting her.

Jack slowed and looked at the woman her looks indicated that she was a dweller of many villages scattered in and around the valley. He didn't want to waste his time so he decided to overlook her and go ahead.

"Sahib, my child is lost, I came here to search him but now I'm lost myself." she stood up and said in haste.

"What do you want?" Jack asked gruffly.

"Please help me searching my kid."

"That is not possible lady right now, I'm in a hurry to go somewhere," said Jack feeling something weird.

"Please help me; the wild beasts shall eat me and my kid."

Jack was in a dilemma, he was finding it hard that a kid could be lost in the vast valley, people around here teach their kids to not to mess with the valley. But if she was right he was risking two human lives just to save one. He decided that the life of hunter wasn't important but solving the mystery behind all previous killings was important. He thought for a while and said, "Tell me where you saw your child last time?"

"This way sir." said the woman gleefully.

Knock Of Death

Manjit was fed up of shooting stray dogs and hyenas who were trying to cross the ditch to eat the goats. But it was all part of the game; he'll have to endure it all to win the wonderful trophies which might appear any time.

Suddenly he sensed that big cats were around and getting close to him silently. He put on his night vision glass and looked around; yes, they were around, too close to his imagination. He smiled and fixed his gun target.

Suddenly he felt a mosquito bite on his neck and rubbed his neck with his thick fingers. He felt dizzy and fell on the ground he was semi-paralyzed, the sting on his neck had injected some sort of poison in his body which has paralyze him. His fear proved to be right, he was really in a fix.

"Buenos días señores........."

He heard a familiar voice which greeted him in Spanish.

Soon the killer trio Carlos Luis, Jose Alejandro and Jorge Eduardo were standing in front of him.

"How are you Karanveer? Greetings from Don Juan, against whom you testified in the federal court and helped FBI to send him away for 15 years. But he is ruling on the Massachusetts Central Jail where he is serving his term. Contract on your head is five years old since you eloped from the States to hide here in India." said one of them.

Manjit really cursed the day when he testified against his own boss, drug lord Don Juan. The FBI offered him a hideout under the witness protection program, but he preferred to live on his own in India in the disguise of a Sikh. But his hunting habit helped these killers to take him out of his hideout.

"Time to say goodbye, you really took a long time to come out of your hideout, we had to get the other hunters killed to protect our pets, the big cats. We had to paralyze them using the Chinese dart guns containing some ancient Chinese poison, rest of the work had to be done by our dear cats, they are fond of us now." said the other foreigner.

Third one whistled hard and all the three big cats come out of the bushes around. They were waving their tales carefully and looking at Manjit and the three standing men simultaneously. The standing men gave them way and they darted at the man on the ground. Rani dug her teeth on his neck and enjoyed the hot blood from his veins. The cub didn't wait; they tore open his stomach and started eating him alive.

In the meantime, the killer trio has vanished in the dark cold night.

End Of The Hunt

"Where is your kid? You are just taking me here and there are you sure your kid is around here?" Jack asked the woman who was sitting behind him on the horse.

"He must be here or near my village." said the woman touching Jack's thigh.

Jack ignored her and asked, "Where is your village?"

"At the northern edge of the valley." replied the woman touching his thigh again.

"Quite far from here," said Jack again ignoring the woman.

"Can you take me to my village?" said the woman holding Jack from behind.

It was enough for Jack, he stopped the horse and pushed the

woman down. She fell on the ground and Jack also came down with her.

"Who are you, woman? What do you want?" asked Jack with a lot of anger.

"Nothing sir some foreigners gave me money to keep you away from the hunter..." she left her sentence incomplete as they both heard the roar of the tigers nearby.

Jack looked at her with disgust and rode his horse to find the origin of the roar.

The moment Jack reaches the hunter's loft the tigers had eaten a big part of the hunter's body.

Jack got down his horse silently and took out his tranquilizing gun and fired three perfect tranquilizing darts at the tigers. They left the half-eaten human body and ran towards the other part of valley but Jack fired other darts which made the tigers unconscious and they fell on the ground.

Jack overlooked them and went close to the hunter to see if there was any sign of life in him but there was none.

After a while he called up all the major TV channels and told them that the man-eaters of the Kali Valley have been subdued.

After that, he took nylon ropes from his leather satchel and tied the tigers' feet carefully.

At the end, he called up the DIG to call the zoo people to take the tigers away.

False Animal Lover

The moment DIG Rahul reached the hunting site the zoo people had caged the tigers and media was covering this event.

"So, you captured the beasts?" asked the DIG to Jack with an ironic gesture.

"Yes, but you let the foreign killers roam around the valley and kill the rest of the hunters," Jack said with a serious tone.

"No, the tigers killed all the hunters, all alike this one......." replied the DIG.

"With the help of the drug syndicate killers."

"Maybe or maybe not, does it make any difference?"

"Yes, it makes a lot of difference, people got killed in this drama of fishing out a witness from his hideout who was under a witness protection program."

"So, you concluded it in this way."

"Am I wrong?"

"What can I say, if foreign people made this land a place to settle their scores, what could we do?"

"They settled their scores but people of our country became their victims."

"People? Or the hunters, who kill innocent animals for their own pleasure?"

"So, you love animals."

"Yes, I do, do you have any problem?"

By that time the sun has risen and the zoo people had loaded the tigers' cages in the zoo trucks. And the media people rushed towards Jack and one of them asked, "Mr Jack the reward on these beasts is rupees one crore, what will you do with that prize money?"

"My daughter wants a good car for her so I'm thinking of purchasing a Mercedes Benz for her."

"So, what happens to your high thinking, you were not interested in the prize money. Now you are dying to collect that reward!" asked the DIG in his mocking voice.

"The man-eaters have been caught alive; they'll be kept in a zoo in high security. What is wrong if I collect the prize money to keep my daughter happy," answered Jack briefly.

The DIG frowned but kept quiet. Jack saw the zoo trucks leaving the valley towards the city zoo. It was a strange misadventure, people got killed and their killers shall entertain kids and other people of the city.

He patted Duke and rode on it silently; Duke started sprinting towards the stead farm. Jack cast a last look at the whole scenario and left. He wanted to catch some sleep before keeping his promise to his daughter who must be waiting for him at the farmhouse.

Raj Verma Art

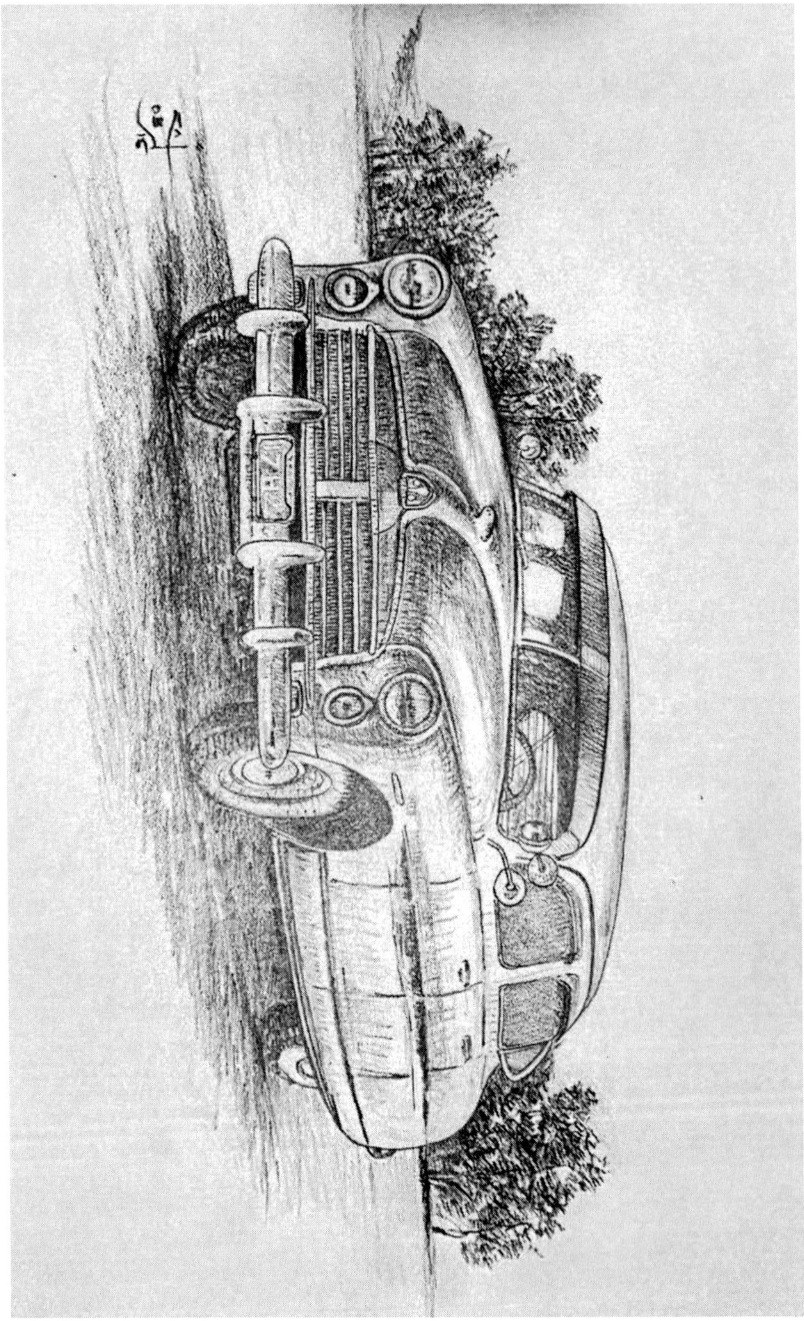

7.12
2014

17.12.2014

Pictures

Front Page

Main Picture : Elizabeth Esguerra Castillo

Left to right-

Arohi, Athrav, Smrutikant Nayak, Promila Bhardawaj

Back Page

First Row

Left to right-

Elizabeth Esguerra Castillo, Charles Darnell, Iram Fatima 'Ashi', Praveen Gola, Shahid Khan, IlonaLakatos

Second Row

Left to right-

Dr Ram Sharma, Dr Sahab Uddin, Dr Ruchida Barman, Kumar Vikrant, Raj Verma, Dr Ratan Bhattacharjee

Third Row

Left to right-

Dr Abhisarika Prajapati, Anurag Sharma, Dr Mausmi Mullick, Dr Priyanka Mathur, Binod Dawadi, Aparna Mukherjee

Pictures used on front, back page covers and inside the book are taken with thank from PIXABAY.COM.